make things fly

Make

things fly

poems about the wind

edited by DOROTHY M. KENNEDY

illustrated by SASHA MERET

MARGARET K. McELDERRY BOOKS

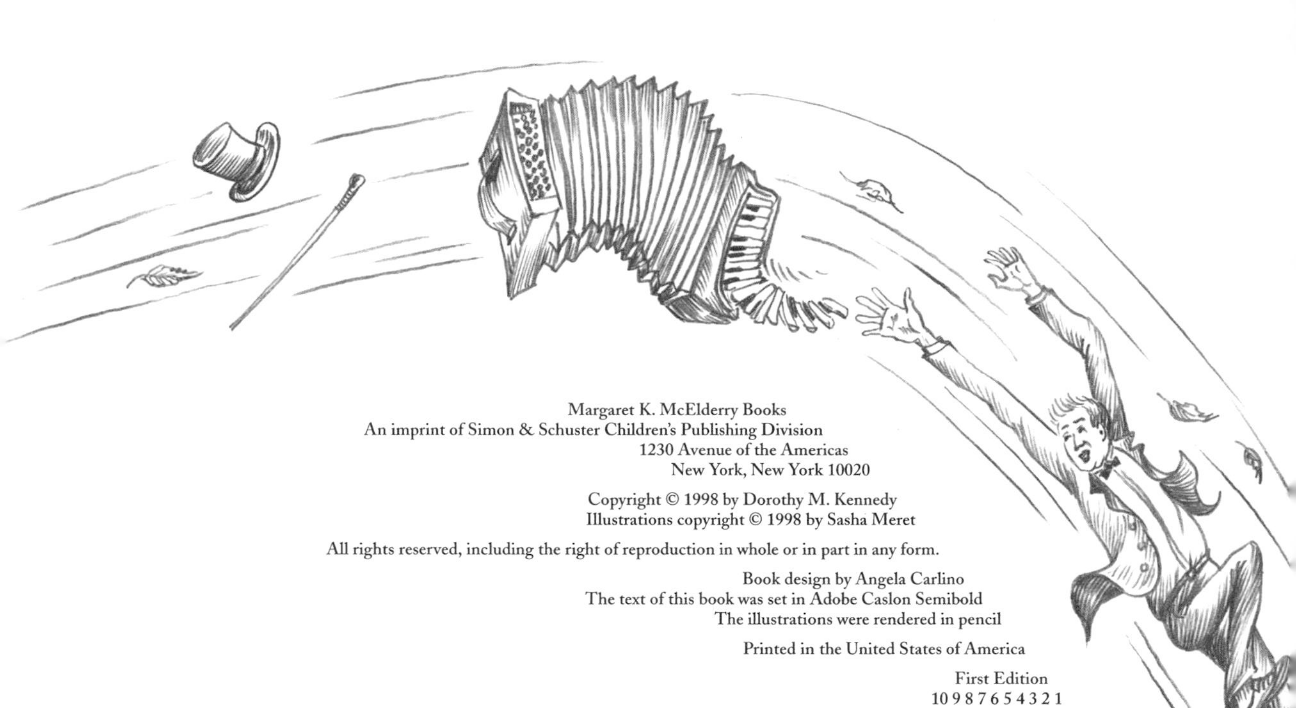

Margaret K. McElderry Books
An imprint of Simon & Schuster Children's Publishing Division
1230 Avenue of the Americas
New York, New York 10020

Book design by Angela Carlino
The text of this book was set in Adobe Caslon Semibold
The illustrations were rendered in pencil

Printed in the United States of America

First Edition
10 9 8 7 6 5 4 3 2 1

Library of Congress Cataloging-in-Publication Data
Make things fly: poems about the wind / edited by Dorothy M. Kennedy; illustrated by Sasha Meret.—1st ed.
p. cm.
Summary: A collection of poems describing the wind by such writers as Lilian Moore, John Ciardi, Christina Rossetti, A. A. Milne, and Eve Merriam.
ISBN 0-689-81544-1
1. Wind—Juvenile poetry. 2. Children's poetry, American. 3. Children's poetry, English.
[1. Wind—Poetry. 2. American poetry—Collections. 3. English poetry—Collections.]
I. Kennedy, Dorothy M. (Dorothy Mintzlaff). II. Meret, Sasha, ill.
PS595.W45M35 1998
811.008'036—dc21
97-13028
CIP AC

In loving memory of my mother and father
—D. M. K.

For Oana, Alexandra, Colin, and Ellis,
who keep me flying
—S. M.

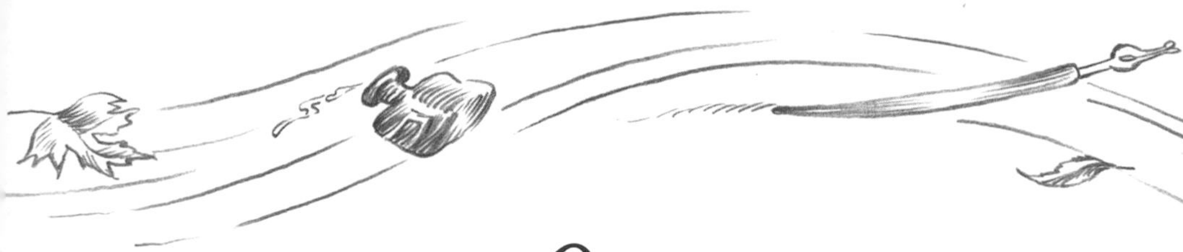

Contents

Wouldn't You?

JOHN CIARDI

If I
Could go
As high
And low
As the wind
As the wind
As the wind
Can blow—

I'd go!

Wind Music

Aileen Fisher

The west wind plays a merry tune
upon the pine all afternoon . . .
the music swells and ebbs.
I wonder if a little breeze,
too small to play upon the trees,
can play on spider webs?

Go Wind

LILIAN MOORE

Go wind, blow
Push wind, swoosh.
  Shake things
  take things
  make things
    fly.

  Ring things
  swing things
  fling things
    high.

Go wind, blow
Push things
whee.
  No, wind, no.
  Not me—
  not *me.*

Tornado

Adrien Stoutenburg

Wind went by with people falling out of it,
and hairpins,
and a barn door swinging without its hinges.
Grass rose in swarms along with nails.
A crow flew upsidedown,
his legs reaching skyward,
and growing longer.

Days that the wind takes over

KARLA KUSKIN

Days that the wind takes over
Blowing through the gardens
Blowing birds out of the street trees
Blowing cats around corners
Blowing my hair out
Blowing my heart apart
Blowing high in my head
Like the sea sound caught in a shell.
One child put her thin arms around the wind
And they went off together.
Later the wind came back
Alone.

Hush-a-Bye Baby

SUNDAIRA MORNINGHOUSE

Hush-a-bye baby
in the tree top
the wind blows the cradle
and my, how it rocks
birds come to whistle
stars bend to gaze
at the pretty brown baby
who spends all her days
rocking in tree tops
dancing in wind
higher and higher
she twirls and spins
an autumn leaf dancing
a chocolate-kiss star
in a sun-sweet forest
of loving arms

Blow, Wind

NORMA FARBER

I watched the waving milkweed tips,
    the soaring sail of thistle.

I thought I saw the wind's own lips
    purse up into a whistle.

Fall Wind

MARGARET HILLERT

I scarcely felt a breath of air;
I didn't hear a sound,
But one small leaf came spiraling
In circles to the ground.

And then the wind began to rise.
I felt it on my face.
It blew my jacket out behind
And made the white clouds race.

It seized the branches of the trees
And shook with might and main.
The leaves poured down upon the earth
Like drops of colored rain.

Crick! Crack!

EVE MERRIAM

Crick! Crack!
Wind at my back.

Snit! Snat!
Snatched off my hat.

Whew! Whew!
It blew and it blew.

Snapped at my ears,
Flapped at my shoes,

And now I've got only
One mitten to lose.

Windy Nights

RODNEY BENNETT

Rumbling in the chimneys,
  Rattling at the doors,
Round the roofs and round the roads
  The rude wind roars;
Raging through the darkness,
  Raving through the trees,
Racing off again across
  The great gray seas.

Windy Nights

ROBERT LOUIS STEVENSON

Whenever the moon and stars are set,
    Whenever the wind is high,
All night long in the dark and wet,
    A man goes riding by.
Late in the night when the fires are out,
Why does he gallop and gallop about?

Whenever the trees are crying aloud,
    And ships are tossed at sea,
By, on the highway, low and loud,
    By at the gallop goes he.
By at the gallop he goes, and then
By he comes back at the gallop again.

Where Would You Be?

KARLA KUSKIN

Where would you be on a night like this
With the wind so dark and howling?
Close to the light
Wrapped warm and tight
Or there where the cats are prowling?

Where would you wish you on such a night
When the twisting trees are tossed?
Safe in a chair
In the lamp-lit air
Or out where the moon is lost?

Where would you be when the white waves roar
On the tumbling storm-torn sea?
Tucked inside
Where it's calm and dry
Or searching for stars in the furious sky
Whipped by the whine of the gale's wild cry
Out in the night with me?

Who Has Seen the Wind?

CHRISTINA ROSSETTI

Who has seen the wind?
  Neither I nor you.
But when the leaves hang trembling,
  The wind is passing through.

Who has seen the wind?
  Neither you nor I.
But when the trees bow down their heads,
  The wind is passing by.

The Unknown Color

COUNTEE CULLEN

I've often heard my mother say,
When great winds blew across the day,
And, cuddled close and out of sight,
The young pigs squealed with sudden fright
Like something speared or javelined,
"Poor little pigs, they see the wind."

Robber Rain/Mischief Wind

J. PATRICK LEWIS

Water gossips
on the roof,
murmuring to the trees—
    I'm Robber Rain,
the thief of deep
dark secrets from the seas.

Snowflakes sparkle
heaven, twinkling softly
as they fly—
    I'm Mischief Wind,
who blustered in
and shoveled out the sky.

Wind on the Hill

A. A. MILNE

No one can tell me,
    Nobody knows,
Where the wind comes from,
    Where the wind goes.

It's flying from somewhere
    As fast as it can,
I couldn't keep up with it,
    Not if I ran.

But if I stopped holding
    The string of my kite,
It would blow with the wind
    For a day and a night.

And then when I found it,
    Wherever it blew,
I should know that the wind
    Had been going there too.

So then I could tell them
    Where the wind goes . . .
But where the wind comes from
    Nobody knows.

Conversation with a Kite

BOBBI KATZ

Come back, come back, my runaway kite!
Come back and play with me!

I'm riding and gliding on whirl-away winds.
I'm going somewhere. Can't you see?

Where are you going, my beautiful kite,
flying so high in the sky?

I'm going to visit the lost balloons
that made little children cry.

When I hold your string, oh my magical kite,
why do I feel the wind in my hand?

The wind is a taste of the sky, my young friend,
that I give to a child of the land.

The Wind

KAYE STARBIRD

In spring, the wind's a sneaky wind,
A tricky wind,
A freaky wind,
A wind that hides around the bends
And doesn't die, but just pretends;
So if you stroll into a street
Out of a quiet lane,
All of sudden you can meet
A smallish hurricane.

And as the grown-ups gasp and cough
Or grumble when their hats blow off,
And housewives clutch their grocery sacks
While all their hairdos come unpinned . . .
We kids—each time the wind attacks—
Just stretch our arms and turn our backs.
And then we giggle and relax
And lean against the wind.

The Wind

JOHN CIARDI

The morning after the night before,
  The wind came in when I opened the door.
It blew the "Welcome" off the mat.
  It blew the fur right off my cat.
It blew my shirttail out of my pants.
  It grabbed the curtains and started to dance
Around and around and around about
  Till I opened a window and kicked it out.

The Wind of Spring

MYRA COHN LIVINGSTON

The wind has picked me up,
Picked me up and out from all the others.
He is blowing me away from April
    Into May.

Wind, who blows the poppy's face to pieces,
Wind, who sweeps the Scotch broom in the air,
Wind, who pulls the juniper's long fingers—
    Blow me out from April
    Into May.

Santa Fe Sketch

CARL SANDBURG

The valley was swept with a blue broom to the west.

And to the west, on the fringes of a mesa sunset,
there are blue broom leavings, hangover blue wisps—
bluer than the blue floor the broom touched
before and after it caught the blue sweepings.

The valley was swept with a blue broom to the west.

Wind Song

LILIAN MOORE

When the wind blows
the quiet things speak.
Some whisper, some clang,
Some creak.

Grasses swish.
Treetops sigh.
Flags slap
and snap at the sky.
Wires on poles
whistle and hum.
Ashcans roll.
Windows drum.

When the wind goes—
suddenly
then,
the quiet things
are quiet again.

Note

WILLIAM STAFFORD

straw, feathers, dust—
little things

but if they all go one way,
that's the way the wind goes.

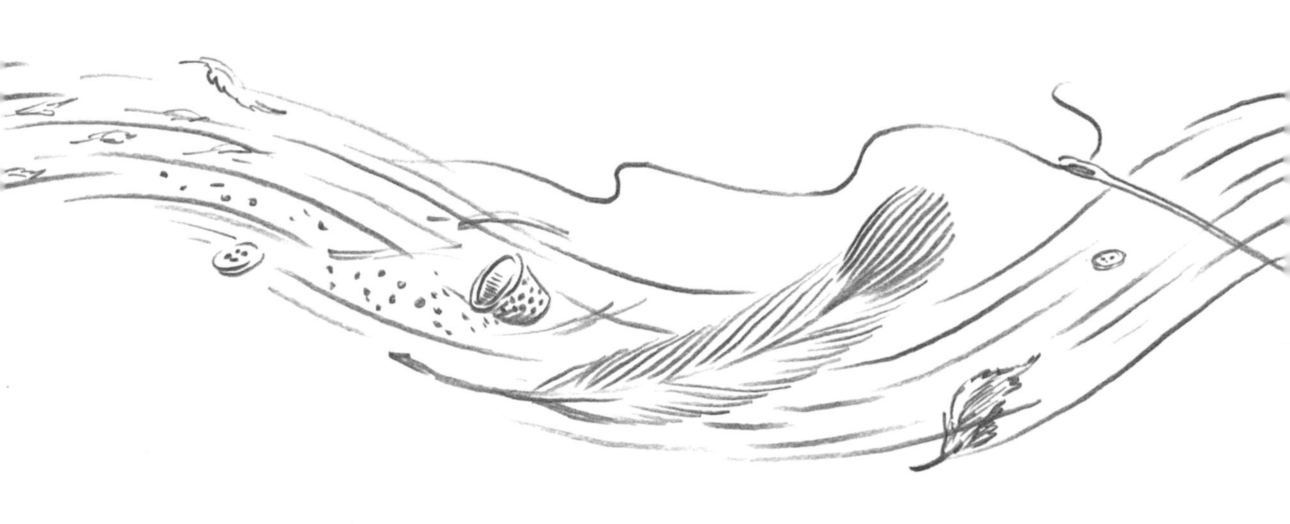

The wind blows paper

HANNAH LYONS JOHNSON

The wind blows paper
High above
The dirty street—
Wild kites without strings

May wind is busy

KAZUE MIZUMURA

May wind is busy
Brushing the robin's tail,
Combing the willow tree,
And whispering to my ear
That summer is near.

The Whisper

JOHN TRAVERS MOORE

"I do not believe in fairies,"
A strange, strange woman said.
"They are bad for children,
Nonsense in the head."

Only the wind
Was heard to blow,
And the whisper in the willows . . .
"Oh-h-h-h!"

What the Wind Said

RUSSELL HOBAN

"Far away is where I've come from," said the wind.
"Guess what I've brought you."
"What?" I asked.
"Shadows dancing on a brown road by an old
Stone fence," the wind said. "Do you like that?"
"Yes," I said. "What else?"
"Daisies nodding, and the drone of one small airplane
In a sleepy sky," the wind continued.
"I like the airplane, and the daisies too," I said.
"What else?"
"That's not enough?" the wind complained.
"No," I said. "I want the song that you were singing.
Give me that."
"That's mine," the wind said. "Find your own." And left.

ACKNOWLEDGMENTS

John Ciardi: "Wouldn't You?" from *You Read to Me, I'll Read to You* by John Ciardi. Copyright © 1962 by John Ciardi. Used by permission of HarperCollins Publishers. "The Wind" from *Mummy Took Cooking Lessons* by John Ciardi. Text copyright © 1990 by Judith C. Ciardi. Reprinted by permission of Houghton Mifflin Co. All rights reserved.

Countee Cullen: "The Unknown Color" reprinted by permission of GRM Associates, Inc., Agents for the Estate of Ida M. Cullen. From the book *Copper Sun* by Countee Cullen. Copyright © 1927 by Harper & Brothers, copyright renewed 1955 by Ida M. Cullen.

Norma Farber: "Blow Wind" by Norma Farber reprinted by permission of Coward, McCann & Geoghegan, Inc. from *Small Wonders,* text copyright © 1979 by Norma Farber.

Aileen Fisher: "Wind Music" from *Out in the Dark and Daylight,* poems by Aileen Fisher. (New York: Harper & Row, 1990.) Reprinted by permission of the author.

Margaret Hillert: "Fall Wind" from *Farther Than Far* by Margaret Hillert (Follett Publishing). Copyright © 1969 by Margaret Hillert. Reprinted by permission of the author who controls all rights.

Russell Hoban: "What the Wind Said" from *The Pedaling Man* by Russell Hoban. Copyright © 1968 by Russell Hoban. Reprinted by permission of Harold Ober Associates Incorporated.

Hannah Lyons Johnson: "The wind blows paper" from *Hello, Small Sparrow* by Hannah Lyons Johnson. Copyright © 1971 by Hannah Lyons Johnson. Reprinted by permission of Lothrop, Lee & Shepard Books, a division of William Morrow and Company, Inc.

Bobbi Katz: "Conversation with a Kite" copyright © 1989 (Random House) from *Poems for Small Friends* by Bobbi Katz. Reprinted with permission of Bobbi Katz.

Karla Kuskin: "Days That the Wind Takes Over" from *Near the Window Tree* by Karla Kuskin © 1975. Reprinted by permission of the author. "Where Would You Be?" from *Dogs & Dragons, Trees & Dreams* by Karla Kuskin. Copyright © 1980 by Karla Kuskin. Used by permission of HarperCollins Publishers.

J. Patrick Lewis: "Robber Rain/Mischief Wind" printed by permission of the author. Copyright © 1998 by J. Patrick Lewis.

Myra Cohn Livingston: "The Wind of Spring" from *A Crazy Flight and Other Poems* by Myra Cohn Livingston. Copyright © 1969 Myra Cohn Livingston. © Renewed 1997 Josh Livingston, Jonah Livingston, and Jennie Livingston. Used by permission of Marian Reiner.

Eve Merriam: *"Crick! Crack!"* from *Blackberry Ink* by Eve Merriam. Copyright © 1985 Eve Merriam. Reprinted by permission of Marian Reiner.

A. A. Milne: "Wind on the Hill" by A. A. Milne from *Now We Are Six* by A. A. Milne. Illustrations by E. H. Shepard. Copyright 1927 by E. P. Dutton, renewed © 1955 by A. A. Milne. Used by permission of Dutton Children's Books, a division of Penguin Books USA Inc.

Kazue Mizumura: "May wind is busy" from *I See the Winds* by Kazue Mizumura. Copyright © 1966 by Kazue Mizumura. Used by permission of HarperCollins Publishers.

Sundaira Morninghouse: "Hush-a-Bye Baby" from *Nightfeathers* by Sundaira Morninghouse. Copyright © 1989. Reprinted by permission of Open Hand Publishing Inc.

John Travers Moore: "The Whisper" from *Cinnamon Seed,* published by Houghton Mifflin Company, 1967.

Lilian Moore: "Wind Song" and "Go Wind" from *I Feel the Same Way* by Lilian Moore. Copyright © 1966, 1967 Lilian Moore. © Renewed 1995 Lilian Moore. "Make Things Fly" from the poem "Go Wind." All of the above used by permission of Marian Reiner for the author.

Carl Sandburg: "Santa Fe Sketch" from *Good Morning, America,* copyright 1928 and renewed 1956 by Carl Sandburg. Reprinted by permission of Harcourt Brace & Company.

William Stafford: "Note" copyright © 1970 William Stafford from *Allegiances* (Harper & Row). Reprinted by permission of The Estate of William Stafford.

Kaye Starbird: "The Wind" from *The Covered Bridge House and Other Poems* by Kaye Starbird. Copyright © 1979 Kaye Starbird Jennison. Used by permission of Marian Reiner.

Adrien Stoutenburg: "Tornado" first appeared in *The Things That Are,* published by Reilly & Lee Company. Copyright © 1964 by Adrien Stoutenburg. Reprinted by permission of Curtis Brown , Ltd.

Index of Authors

INDEX OF TITLES

Index of First Lines